Breaking free

Breaking Free

Rishi Mendez

Published by Rishi Mendez, 2024.

BREAKING FREE

First edition. November 26, 2024.

Copyright © 2024 Rishi Mendez.

ISBN: 979-8230860242

Written by Rishi Mendez.

DEDICATION :

The irony of pain is that you want to be comforted by the one who hurt you .

Dedicated to the countless souls who have endured the storms of emotional abuse . Find the strength to step away from these dark shadows and embrace the peace that comes with freedom from tormentors.

To those who now walk the path of no contact , and chose solitude over suffocation , know that you are not alone . Breaking free from the chains of toxic love isn't cowardice . It reveals your capacity for self preservation . The pain of breakup and self imposed no contact phase in your life will lead you to new beginnings , to healing and the life you deserve .

This story offers a realistic view of the consequences and provides a beacon of hope , solace and few strategies of how to successfully move on .

PROLOGUE :

In a world where hearts are broken and longs for healing , this book explores what I have felt everyday in my journey of self imposed No Contact .

To all the brave survivors who have chosen your battles wisely .You are escaping the aura of persons with their myopic superiority complex which ironically stemmed from their inferiority complex . You are entitled to live your life in this planet without having an anxiety attack everyday in their presence. You need to sleep tight , without nightmares waking you up , and then struggling to fall back to sleep at 3 am .

You given your best . You were always listening . But all you got was dark brooding silence . Sometimes , you got looks that mouthed ' why are you still alive ' ? Now it's up to you to find the answer . Just go . No goodbyes . Just leave .

What you need then , is to look the other way . How's that courage ? , you might ask . It's courage, because not everyone can do it . Does it make any sense to you, to survive the silent suffocating grip ? . It is courage , to sever the chains of abuse . It takes courage to end the cycle of manipulation . How is that an excuse to continue enduring it Would you be happy living like that ?

Do not regret anything that happened . Do not blame yourself . We humans want to make connections to something and want contact with people . That's because it's our human instinct, hard wired into our genetic codes . So while we journey through life , we focus on that instinct , we get into relationships , which sometimes do not work out . They drain us physically and emotionally . Initially you thought that , this exhaustion , that's something which happens from human to human during relationships. But now we know better . It's called abuse .

1

Everything passes , and when it does you will see that , it wasn't much . Dare to choose the agony of no contact over the illusion of love ? . That decision will mark your rebirth . You will reclaim your power , your clarity of mind , the freedom you deserve and eventually finding peace and calm in the aftermath of this storm .

It transforms you in the midst of pain , anger , hopelessness . And finally you reach the shores of power and calm after passing through the crossroads of shattered trust and lies , where you will be determined to find your own strength as if you were a ship that braved the stormy seas,

I have walked this path with you, The pain is real . But in the end the calm , is your victory, Here you will find how to love yourself, and find the strength to let go,

This book will serve you as a lighthouse to dock to and heal , may the winds of change guide you to this lighthouse with your broken heart , reminding you here , that we have the power to rewrite our story and claim happiness again .

The author can be reached on
hellorishimendez@gmail.com

TABLE OF CONTENTS
CHAPTERS

Chapter One

DONT REMINISCE , THERE S NOTHING THERE

The city view faded in the window as my flight took off and moved me further away from the chaos that had gripped my life for too long. As the aircraft climbed and gained altitude, every mile felt like shedding a layer of the past, peeling off the weight of meaningless words, distressing control, the carefully crafted manipulation. I wasn't just leaving this city; I was leaving a version of myself behind.

As the flight landed in this semi urban town , nestled in the hills, far from the reach of anyone who knew me , I felt the suffocating thoughts slowly ebb .The air was different here . So cool, crisp, and pure. The wind whispered secrets to the trees, and for the first time in years, I felt at peace. Basically it's the same job , but at a somewhat remote branch location , not so populated . This branch required only what I was ready to give: solitude, effort, and time.

The apartment provided to me by the firm had a mostly functional layout . It was up to me to make it a cozy space . I was thankful that it was located close to the sea side and that it was furnished . The living area was large , full of sunlight and open spaced with a sliding glass door leading to a ground level balcony facing the sea in the distance . The whole place was painted in pale lavender . A medium sized plush grey sofa large enough to take a nap and a wall mounted flat screen TV and a wooden coffee table .

A small bedroom with a large window and sheer curtains , a queen sized white bed , a tiny built in white wardrobe holding extra linen and bedding and a tiny nightstand with a mirror . The white kitchen with a small refrigerator, a microwave and an electric stove top immediately drew me in . It held a small dining table with four chairs , just like my family home . This can double up as my work station while I use the laptop . A large sea shell sat in the center of the table , like a friend . I loved that .

The bathroom is spotlessly clean with a dedicated shower area , a simple vanity and mirror . I discarded the plastic creeper . I will set up my own creeper . Not bad though . A simple welcoming space .

At night, as the wind howled softly, memories of him may sometimes creep in. There was a pull, a faint echo of nostalgia that tugged at me. I'd remember his charm, the way he'd made me laugh . That was before the darkness set in. But then, I would remind myself that those moments were fleeting, it was mere illusions in the shadow of his true self. I had seen his mask slip too many times. Enough to realize that my world was not a real one there .

The night was thick with memories of when we were together , laying side by side , forgetting the outside world . The soft glow of the moon bathing us in silver light , completely oblivious to everything , turning everything into a dream .

The way he caressed the warm skin. How many nights my breath mingled with his. In that moment, it was like we were always meant to be there. Even the stars seemed brighter on those nights.

We spoke little in bed because words were not that necessary. He and I will remember such nights for the rest of our lives. The pulse of time crawled through our fingers. Those hours, we really slowed down time. Savoring every touch, every whispered laugh, as if trying to seal it forever .

In those nights the smell of my body mingled with the smell of his cigarette. It still exists. It's alive in my mind . It was just chemistry more than love. I know that now. I knew such nights would not last. It was the painful knowledge that passion like this was too bright to survive the dawn. But in those stolen hours , those nights spent together outside of time, we were in a magical world. For him it was nights of lust . For me a false sense of security . Without realizing that , believed so blindly, as if I had no basic level of IQ.

The pangs of loneliness would sometimes rise, but they would no longer scare me. Instead, I will embrace them, recognizing that this solitude was a gift. It was the space I needed to heal. Each day, the grip of the past will loosen a little more. Each moment alone will become just a reminder that I was no longer under his control. I was free.

The wind, which not long ago felt cold and biting in the city I had left , now wrapped around me like a gentle embrace. It carried the promises of tomorrow , ones I had written for myself. I have found peace here , even if it would be fragile at times, and I will hold onto it like a lifeline.

Here, in this quiet place far from the memories, I will rebuild my life . The nostalgia still would come , I will hurt , but one day , it will no longer hurt. One day it would be just a reminder of what I had left behind and what I would finally become.

This night and all nights , I will keep my routine simple yet sacred. I moisturized my hands and feet . Removed my eye makeup. Then night cream on my face. It was a habit. Then like every day, I read my little prayers. It was mainly for my ancestors. For their peace and guidance in my life.

I sipped on a cup of camomile tea . It's warmth filled the hollow spaces of my soul . Where I had dug out and discarded the stored lies given to me . Then I lighted a soft-scented candle and curled up under a woven blanket, the kind that felt to me like home. A book rested on my lap, though tonight I knew I would barely read a page. I let the quiet hum of nature lull me into a different kind of restfulness.

No more waiting for the footsteps that once echoed too loudly in my life , the footsteps that stomped on my heart . No more pretending to be someone I wasn't. My heart slowed as the stars twinkled outside the window, a gentle reminder that peace could be quiet, still, and it could be deeply mine.

CHAPTER TWO

The first daybreak without you

The dawn breaks . The world is awake and vibrant as if nothing happened. But for me the world feels silent and devoid of colors . Morning sun brought with it a warmth that seemed to seep into my soul . I woke peacefully today , no longer jolted by anxiety or the sharp edge of thoughts about what's the torture of today

My God , I wanted you to know , that I made it . I thought the world had stopped for me when I hurt this way , I thought it stopped when am in love too. And now I thought the world stopped for me when in a breakup . I thought it stopped for me when am sick . But now I realize , the worlds stops only when you want it to .

My soul , you picked me up from the storm and brought me back to life . I have taken and I have given . I loved and I hated . For a long time . But now I got it sorted . We did it together . My God , now I want you to know , that am stronger as you wanted . Only you could turn me into the way I am now .

A moment of my weakness , will be a moment of opportunity for others . Sometimes you need a shot of a kind of motivation . One that will remind me of what I tend to forget ! That in order to move a mountain , you need to first clear the small stones out of the way .

The sunlight shone through the curtains, golden and soft . It was just me, breathing in the freedom of a beautiful morning. I stepped out onto the balcony , feeling the stone floor beneath my bare feet, and welcomed the simplicity of the day. The weight on my shoulders now seemed light , and in their place was the promise of this new life I had willingly created. I was free to be exactly who I was, and in that, finally is a peace that no one could take away .

An erotic slideshow of my life with my partner and now ex lover , is parading in front of my mind . It's all in vivid sensual detail . Hell , even dreams aren't this clear in details . Strange that even though I walked out and my mind has rejected him , the body hasn't rejected yet . It's a traitor . My lips missed the hard biting kisses . He's not the only one in the world who can kiss like that . I said to myself .

I missed the sweet nothings of every night . I may miss that though , until the end . I won't blame myself for that .I thought life will only get better without the lies. Why am I not feeling better ? I feel scared to face my day . But it's a Sunday , I can take my time . My coffee as always ,is my life saver. I still feel full , from the lies perhaps ? Or the discovery ? Or both ? Nauseous. Didn't ever want to wake up without you in this life. But it kills me . Will this pain go away ? I will make it go away . It will get better I promise myself. Be kind to yourself , I reminded myself.

My luggage still sits in the hall. Unpacked. Will I survive this day ? I will hold my head up and arrange my apartment to sustain my single life . Yes , I walked out . My life is bigger than this person . I was happy before I met him . I will find it again. Switched on my TV , I need to hear any voice talking, just like a drone .

Humming , I go through the motions of making my apartment cheery . I had planned it well . Transferred to this quiet sea side town which is quiet and somewhat obscure. Well suited to my minimalist life style .

I follow the minimalistic lifestyle . I don't like to buy un necessary things . Whatever I buy , it should serve its purpose . I buy functional but stylish clothes for work. I also own some casual evening wear . Some moderately luxurious party wear . Footwear for office , evenings and for walking . Soft slip ons for home . A small box of differently styled jewelry to mix and match with outfits . A moisturizer, concealer , eyeliner and lip gloss . That's it . This lifestyle gives me peace of mind . When I replace new seasonal clothes , I give away the previous ones to charity .This way I keep my home and my mind clutter free .

The squawking of sea gulls, not so bad . Infinitely better than the drone of lies and the unreasonable demands day in and day out. My home looks beautiful . I am undiscoverable here now . Distance feels so real . Am gonna be okay . Really . By brain now starts the slideshow of memories. No I won't give in to that.

I put on a summer dress and my " feel good ponytail " . Moisturizer on my face to shield against the sun . Light pink lip gloss on my lips . A touch of an eyeliner on my eyebrows . I put on my walking shoes , wore jeans and a purple top and headed outside to explore.

The town hall , the sea shore , the white church reflecting the sun . I roam until I am thirsty and hungry . Really hungry. Am I healing so soon ? No , I won't get my hopes up. My eyes search the pavement outside the restaurant. Who am I searching for? I closed that chapter. I am not going back.

Next , my eyes scanned the row of shops and businesses . My intention was to find a ladies hair saloon . I believe that after a break up , it is necessary to get a make over . Trim the hair into a new hair style to suit your face . It is guaranteed to change your look . It will change it for the better . I think that most of the women know this already . I found a good saloon . Within an hour , my hairstyle changed . This haircut made me younger and vibrant than before . . On the way back , I purchased light color rose gloss . I will change my lipstick color too . No more red lipstick . just beautiful pink gloss . That done , I got into the nearby cafe and got myself a hot chocolate on the go.

The wonderful thing about Cocoa . whether you eat it as a chocolate or whether you drink it as hot chocolate, it uplifts your mood in five minutes . It makes you ready to take on the harsh world . Your confidence up to the sky then . That's why I love chocolate or hot chocolate . Another dish that gives me pleasure is a dish in which dates are stuffed inside pastry and baked . It's called Mamool . It's an

Arabian sweet . It uses very little sugar . I know to make it at home too .

Did I tell you why I left ? It's because I got shell shocked by the real face after the carefully constructed mask slipped.

My discovery that the partner who really loved me had this sick craving for attention and thrived on constant texting and then sexting with whoever was available . Age barrier wasn't a problem . Even to teens online , by creating fake identities . Even lonely wives of other people , enticing them into the dark world of lies and deceit . Modern day diagnosis of this behavior calls it looking for endless supply of people to validate them 24/7 .

I was told it's a behavior of covert narcissists . A condition of which I never heard much about . Once they have you in their pocket for good, they seek the thrill of novelty elsewhere, while never ever letting you go , as you are their primary dependable so called supply who loves them to the moon and back .

Our love life and chemistry was great , but then why ? It was a sickness , a quest for something forbidden something that society considers taboo. Complimenting others lavishly when I was given just breadcrumbs . It took a while to realize it was just breadcrumbs .Yes, it was a sickness. I was blissfully unaware if anything physical took place . But I think not. The relentless demands in bed almost everyday rules out that possibility.

Then discovering that everything was copied and tracked for five years from my devices, scrutinized , judged, and revenged upon , secretly. Discovering that my partner was addicted to porn which explained the bizarre physical needs in bed day and night . Which actually triggered me to leave .

At home now and a short nap without the need to service this trash for hours in bed . Am free finally . Or Am I ?

Evening and then sunset , the dreaded time when you think about all that's lost . No I didn't lose . Instead of sitting on his feet and servicing his body while he sipped on a glass of rum, now my time is mine. I bet he has no one now to service his body like that. Cheerfully I open the TV , set it on mute just to see the moving images and then put on some rock music , the kind that's far away from love , loss and betrayal. Oh that feels good .

I sliced an apple and had it with a herbal tea. In bed , the stormy mind takes hold again. Did he move on ? Really ? Well there's no way of knowing . Who cares . I won't stalk his social media and he can't stalk mine. I made sure of that.

I tried to sleep. But the memory of his lips on mine ,burning me like fire. His voice whispers. kiss my lips now babe . I want it now. Then he opened my lips with his tongue. I want to touch you tonight. Your whole body . Yes I whispered. It continued through the long hours of the night. Not letting me sleep. Now I know what it is. Only lust for my body. Not love.

It took me this long to let go . It was easier for me to linger than to let go . To give up the dreams I built . Not because I was brave . But because I was afraid to let go .

Will this pain ever subside ? Will this ache ever fade ? The traitor in me tempted me to unblock him from my phone. Pain panic and hopelessness consumed my thoughts. I shook it off . I reminded myself of the reasons I went no contact in the first place . Self preservation is now my top priority. Self love my next step . Self respect prevailed and I drowned in sleep.

CHAPTER THREE
HEALING IS WEIRD

Wide awake. A sound drifting in from somewhere near . It's a song . The song makes me miss someone who was never mine. Yesterday I was holding on to your thoughts. Today I ll let you go . Crazy though , how much I still love you . Every day and night why do I still love you so much .I hated myself .

Am a traitor to my self respect , to even think this way. Why fight for something that'd not worth it ? What's meant for my energy will eventually find me . You are not meant for my energy. That's it .

Just for today I'll be philosophical. This past journey was a long journey . With its downs and it ups . It had its good things and a lot of bad . The next journey I'll make it like a movie . I will direct it . I will screenwriter it . It will have actors only chosen by me . Apparently , my choice of actors in my last journey wasn't perfect .

The important thing is , that this journey isn't over . There are several paths each with a new starting point that I will have to choose. Seeing it like that made me feel better

Driving to work . Still these thoughts are smoking in my head like ominous black clouds . I ll show you what you really lost . I'll make better memories . That will override yours . Reaching the new company branch premises, I put my best foot forward . Feels good to see vast airy sunlit spaces . Friendly faces waved. No one seemed inquisitive or curious . Life is good .

After my work , while On my way home I stopped at the cafe . Collected the hot chocolate on the go. Spotting a guy seductively smiling at me , I hurried out . No way . At home now , I sipped hot chocolate trying to take stock of my situation. Single , with a new locality to get used to, no more breakfast in bed , no more waking up to the warmth of a man , no more good morning kiss , (oh it was fake anyway)

I never had any trouble getting him to achieve an erection. In a few minutes I made him ready for love.

He always moaned in pleasure when my tongue touched his shaft. It always gave me more confidence. We made love all night, talking love and sweet words. How can men have so many faces ? I can't believe the acting even though these memories make me uncomfortable. After a long night we both used to head to the shower to clean up. There too he showed his desire. He was just so crazy for me . I was the madness that flowed in his veins.

I have to start dating . But slowly . For now I have to complete the tail end of a project . It's a new branch . Gotta impress . Though Missing the other side . But not dying already . But this shit hurts I know . But it can never hurt my spirit . I will rise faster than a Phoenix. I am happy that I escaped a mind boggling self centered trash with temper tantrums like a five year old . Am not a captive of your crazy world . Go crazy yourself , don't count me in anymore .

Hitting the bed . Zero feelings . Will I ever touch a man in reciprocation of desire , again ? Will I bloom like a flower under the rain , again ? I felt like my life was like gone under the earth already .

To all the brave survivors who chose your battles wisely . You have given your best . You were always listening . But all you got was meditative dark silence . Sometimes , looks that mouthed ' why are you still alive ' . Now it's up to you to find the answer . Just leave . No goodbyes .

What you need then , is to look the other way. How's that courage , you might ask . It's courage, because not everyone can do it. Does it make any sense to you, to survive the silent suffocating grip . It is courage , to sever the chains of abuse . It takes courage to end the cycle of manipulation . How is that an excuse to continue enduring it . Would you be happy living like that ?

Do not regret anything that happened . Do not blame yourself for wanting to make connections to something , and to want contact with people . That's because it's our human instinct, hard wired into our genetic codes . So while we journey through life , we focus on that instinct , we get into relationships , which sometimes do not work out . They drain us physically and emotionally. Initially you thought that , this exhaustion , that's something which happens from human to human during relationships. But now we know better . It's called abuse .

Everything passes when it does you will see that it wasn't much . Would you dare now , to choose the brief misery of no contact over the long illusion of love . That decision will be your rebirth . You will reclaim your power , the sanity of mind , the freedom you all deserve and eventually finding peace and calmness in the aftermath of this storm .

Sunrise. Another day . I will make this day beautiful. Today I will burn all the clothes that I ever wore out with you . Perhaps I will smile back seductively at the disturbingly masculine man at the cafe who has already given rather suggestive smiles .

What I wanted in a weird way was a guy that has two facets of personality . The one that fulfills the friend zone and the one that is fiercely loving and masculine , complete with jealousy , possessiveness and what not .Well this type exists only in fantasies. Either they are the friend zoning angle or they are the friends with benefits angle. Can't have both . Saying this to myself, I went through the daily rituals at work. Clocking in . Facing clients . Facing life . I delved deep into work .

At home , dreading to get into the shower again , thinking that I will never shower with you again .

What's this ? It's a wave of madness and memories .

Stay put . I am not going back . Be thankful that the tormentor is gone . I felt my body in the shower . I felt it ready for love . I heard the fake words in my ears spoken in our showers together. I missed it

. Thus in the shower , my heart broke all over again , it broke into a million pieces, like the millions of water droplets that cleansed me .

CHAPTER FOUR

STRANGERS WITH MEMORIES

Another day, a sense of relief as if a weight had lifted off my shoulders. No more second guessing myself to try to please someone who was never satisfied. But why a lingering sadness . A feeling of emptiness. My aunt had told me a few days ago .... " mourn him as if you would mourn a partner who has passed away...go through the tears , the despair, the longing , the finality , then put it behind you ". Easier said than done , but she had a point . When you think of it that way , you feel the finality .

For the first time I thought philosophically. We are born alone . We should be happy in our own company . If people play you in the life journey , don't ever cry . Smile because love happened to you , then remove them mercilessly. I found myself crying like a teen on my way to work. It's called mourning , it's called closure . I said to myself .

The most powerful move you can make against an abusive or narcissist partner is no move at all . The narcissist is hoping you would say something unpleasant, because once you do , the whole aspect of the conversation is flipped . The focus now changes to what you just said . Subject effortlessly diverted . What they did to you is moved out of everyones attention .

Don't think that They don't know full well what they are doing . They know well that they are hurting you. They may not know why they are doing it . But they know what hurts you . They just don't have the ability to care . Don't get all bothered by trying to show them that they have hurt you .So when they give you these chances to hurt them it's a trap . You don't need a confession from an abuser . Walking away could be the best choice you can make .

After work , I went for a walk on a quiet street . Breathing in the fresh air and feeling a strange calm hearing the rustle of the trees that lined the little street . Got into the bakers and got my favorite jam filled biscuits and a small baguette for next days breakfast .

At home . I played my favorite playlist and ate a few of the biscuits . Time for some foot care . I had a small electric foot spa. Round shape. I put water and aromatic salts in it and soaked my feet in it. It was so relaxing . It gives gentle vibrations to the feet. I felt my fatigue disappear. The music is good. What a peace to be away from the city.

While in the shower the pine like needles of water fell like sensual rain on targeted places. I felt strange thoughts coming . I was wet , but not entirely from the shower. I heard the phone ringing. The missed call was from a VOIP call. It was him trying to reach me . I won't fall for that . I knew that he missed me . He missed the sex . The care and the love. I now know that also , it's akin to the feeling when a child misplaces his favorite toy . He loses interest in all other new toys and searches the one that got out . Just because he wants it back in his collection . It's a pattern .

These first few days are the hardest . I know that . If I can survive this , I can reclaim my life . It wasn't an easy journey , but I did have the courage to break free . I created distance , thus reducing the chances of ever running in to each other . Let them live in all their glory with their tribe , who justifies and condones everything they do . In life it's important to know when to stop arguing with people who have done you wrong . Simply let them be wrong . Leave it at that . If they ever think that this sort of abuse leaves you feeling stuck , ashamed , lost , alone , powerless ,crazy , devalued , embark, and guilty , prove them wrong at any cost . Which is what am doing now .

Understand that toxic people never change . They just change their victims . Seriously , how can you navigate discussion with someone who is complete self centered ? Even if a victim forgets and moves on , the victims nerves certainly remember the abuse .

Sometimes family is the culprit . A bunch of narcissists and abusers in there who practically derailed your life . Do not ever include them in your healing . When you heal from this , it doesn't mean that they will stop doing it . You have just made it possible for them not to hurt you anymore . But the abuse goes on . It's now directed at new victims .

To all who are undergoing the pain of self imposed no contact , do all you can to move to another locality if possible, where your toxic partner' s smear campaign cannot reach your ears , Trust the instincts , that made you take this step and never look back on that road of bygones. If you do pick up that unknown call, trust me you lose more value in their eyes .

And then at night comes the hard part . The touch missed from your lover . When you remember it , your body builds up the heat in degrees. I found myself throwing off my clothes and pretending . Missing how I used to sit on his belly and giving him the hot sunsets and nights of his life. At weekends it went on like a marathon . Did I really do all that for this player ? What a waste of my talents .

Some sunsets he asked her to be commando. To wear only just a top and a skirt. Nothing else. She always obeyed him. Making him happy was always my priority. As he drank a glass of rum at sunset, I sat at his feet and served him. In every possible way. But why these two fake faces? I will never know why. I think it's a disease. When I was menstruating, I used to serve his needs with my mouth. What an ungrateful creature, I thought.

Reaching out to pick up the lifelike toy which was gifted to me last birthday by him , I quelled that treacherous urge and the nostalgia , in the next five minutes . See ? , it's easy . I told myself .

No contact phase is not so hard , once you focus on keeping your decision intact . Everything else can be sorted out . I felt like a garden that suddenly bloomed again after a drought .

Never ever disclose your location. If you disclose where you are , you are again giving them a chance to disrespect you, and devalue you as a human being. You will then enter a lifetime of misery with this delusional person , who will put you through another cycle that never ends .

In the new office branch already guys have their eyes on the newcomer . No way am going to take up someone on the rebound , or should I ? No harm in having some no strings fun though. I projected myself as a cheerful but private person . So far it has worked out . Time and time again I feel to revenge . But I will not do it. The fact that abusers and their tribes have no access to me is revenge enough .

I began to fill my days with this new routine . This was something I hadn't had control over in past years. My mornings and evenings , before arriving here , were taken over by the preferences and demands of an abuser . Now I cherished morning walks through the sea side paths, inhaling the scent of the sea , and the soft chirps of birds now replaced the drone of lies .

If I woke a little late , these paths I took were filled with the sounds of fishermen and boats , bringing in all kinds of live seafood. Sometimes I stopped to watch the merchandise . Squids , swordfish , crabs , shrimps and soles , touted as catch of the day . I wasn't much of a seafood enthusiast. But it was very satisfying to watch .

At home , I even unpacked my books , and arranged them in a niche under the television stand , I picked up on my daily reads and slowly, I began to feel whole , I felt a purpose . I turned over in my bed and tried to sleep .

CHAPTER FIVE
THE FUN IS BACK AND ITS NOT FROM YOU

I woke up with another bout of sensual nostalgia . I looked at the toy . I knew then that I was back on track . For days I never felt wet. Another round wouldn't hurt . No it didn't hurt . It calmed my sunrise , calmed my usual panic attack waking up alone . That , a quick shower and a coffee , I was ready to face the day. I looked at the phone . Several missed VOIP calls at night . How would I hear it . I was dead to the world after relaxing .

I decided that this weekend I will invite the seductive guy from the cafe , and the friend zone guy from my office and his older sister over for dinner. If the seductive guy gives a seductive smile tonight , he s in . He looked so transparent . I should take a chance . In the shower I felt beautiful again , bold to take on the harsh world , ready to maintain this hell of no contact at any cost .

Where did all this masculine type of energy come to me ? I wondered . I know the answer now . Trauma . Women like me having had to be extremely independent in life , with the men in our life who is not confident enough in their own masculinity, who lie , betray and cover up like cowards . There are so many women I know who have this defensive type of masculine energy . I belong to that club now . We all probably never had a man who created a safe space for us to show our naturally inherent feminine traits . We were literally forced to steer the ship .

Tomorrow is a weekend. Tackling the most urgent jobs took all of the morning at work. At lunch time I had fresh fruit with the friend zone guy and invited him over for the weekend dinner with his sister. Who else is there , he asked . For now only three of us , but let's see , I replied.

Evening I hit the cafe for my hot chocolate take away . The seductive guy was seductive as usual but the seductive smile was missing . What ? Did you lose your nerve already ? I decided to take the game into my own hands and help him out to deliver the seductive smile. I sat down innocently with my hot chocolate on the table that was facing him , instead of taking my drink home . Our eyes met. I gave a slight hint of a smile and deliberately looked for a ring on his finger. That worked. " I am not married " He said . Can I join your table ? From there seductive guy and me took off . Innocent banter . I felt comfortable and not on edge . Thank you my Lord , for this friend .

The first thing I asked was the zodiac sign. It was Scorpio. What a relief ! I would have run a mile if it was Aries. I was a Libra. Ah the diplomatic romantic Libra , he smiled. The seductive heart melting smile.

He took me to the fresh market. I needed to buy ingredients for the weekend dinner. I bought chicken, butter, beef, milk, tomatoes, cucumbers, onion , cream, tortillas, some stuff was already stocked in my fridge . Rest I shall buy online . Also bought two sparkling grape wines. Then we went to the seafood market. Bought clams and tuna from there. Scorpio helped me choose fresh seafood.

After finishing our purchases, Scorpio took me to a street cafe. We bought sandwiches filled with delicious sauces. A chicken sandwich for him and an eggplant and potato sandwich for me. I love vegetarian food . Although I know how to prepare most non-vegetarian dishes, I prefer vegetarian. I have been like that since childhood. That was impossible for Scorpio. Discussing about this we laughed hard as he walked me the rest of the way to the parking lot . There , I came to know that he rides a bike .

While I started my car , he started his bike . Scorpio waved as I drove by . He seemed over the moon when I invited him for next day dinner. But the smile turned lopsided when I said there were going to be two of my colleagues for dinner . What an expressive face that conveys exactly what's felt inside , as opposed to the mask I was dealing past years.

At home , my routine . I soaked my hands and legs with moisturizer . Removed my eye makeup . Then night cream on my face . Camomile tea. Like I do every day , I read my short prayers for my ancestors . Please guide me ancient souls . I know that you're all out there .

The inevitable thoughts . Is he even getting a boner without porn nowadays ? He loved her ability to make him erect even after playing and riding on his stomach like a marathon . I think that's why primarily we were together . Some take boner pills to perform better. But when he was with me there was no need for that ever .

What a fool I am, to believe and accept all that. A word to everyone reading this. Don't give sex endlessly. Know when to give and when to hold back . A commodity that is always abundant loses its value and price. By commodity I mean sexual services. Not people or partners . I realized it too late , this fundamental theory . I guess along with the lies and betrayal , this reason of taking for granted too , was pivotal in leaving that life ultimately.

I thought about the menu for the guest dinner. To put it mildly, I know how to cook well. Most of the recipes I know belong to my Anglo Indian community. If I prepare it well, they are incredibly tasty dishes. I think my guests will enjoy my home cooked food.

That night I slept soundly after ordering online all of the remaining groceries and ingredients I needed for the weekend dinner .

CHAPTER SIX
A LIGHTHOUSE

After office I took my hot chocolate on the go as usual . Scorpio was not on his seat in the cafe . Perhaps he was grooming for the dinner ? Guys do that you know . Parking my car at the front of my building , I skipped on to home . One of the things I learned early in life , was to cook staple and authentic Anglo meals which reflected my Anglo culture.

I set about a feast . For the starters an oyster soup with fresh oysters purchased from the sea food market near me , served with warm rolls . Mashed potatoes shaped into cutlets with ground beef and grilled. Soft Tortillas stuffed with grilled chicken , cheese , lettuce , onion and ripe tomatoes , a Shrimp and mushroom stir fried dish with sliced carrots and green sweet peppers , sprinkled liberally with freshly ground pepper , an Anglo salad with skinned tomatoes , cucumber and ice berg lettuce dressed in olive oil and herbs , paired it all with a large bowl of soft steamed buttered long grain rice .

For a simple dessert , Homemade Chocolate chip cookies and peanut butter cookies with Lemon Green Tea and Jasmine Tea to round it off . My small home smelled of wonderful home cooked food . I felt exhausted , after all the cooking . But I was happy to find purpose . Happy that all these good people are going to visit me , and that I succeeded in getting a few well meaning friends.

My guests filled up my house with laughter. They tucked into the food like hungry kids . Scorpio looked incredibly dashing in jeans and a skin fitting shirt . With my permission , he had brought his Labrador and everyone bonded with him immediately , even my friend zone guy and his sister looked good . The food all but disappeared . Three hours passed . I was happy . I was not alone in this world . The dog surprisingly , lay at my feet. He must have loved the beef patty I cooked for him . I was good with dogs . I cared for three German shepherds in my student years . I stroked the contented dog . Life was good .

Except Scorpio, all the others left . Scorpio done the dishes. I was grateful . Scorpio suggested watching a movie on my subscription channel and I agreed . The dog cuddled up to me again and half way through the movie I cuddled up to Scorpio without any other thoughts except a human company . In this time , I made it clear to him that we are just friends and maybe just maybe we could become friends with benefits gradually ,but with no promises now . Definitely with no heartbreak or feelings involved.

But right now I was not going to enter a relationship on the rebound . I just wanted to float a while . A friendship boat , that's all I wanted now . He understood and it looked like he was ready to wait if and when it happens , if it ever happens .

That night I knew that he too , was a victim of a heartbreak two years ago . The movie ended and we shared the necessary details of ourselves , lingering over a cup of coffee . It was one am when he left with the adorable dog . It looked like we both found a lighthouse to dock our ships, even though temporarily.

I now know , that no contact is not the end of the world. I need not wait for a Prince Charming . It's now instincts and the gut feeling that can serve as a compass. If your gut feels you are doing it right , go for it. There is no Prince Perfect out there too. No one is perfect .

Take every chance of happiness that you get . If you feel a distinct red flag waving at you , pull off immediately. Since no contact is a trial period , do not give your heart to anyone , if you do , then is a chance you may get knifed in the same place as before .

I did not find a haven in these new people . I know that. Yet there is comfort and friendship out there. It won't come searching for you . Don't be blind to it . Don't mourn forever . You have to look out for it , identify it , give it a try , take a chance and bond with it . It's there . For you and me . You can unlearn all those . But you can't afford , to let this pass by you .

CHAPTER SEVEN
A NEW STORY OF TRUST

The sea breeze had a way of pulling the weight off her shoulders as she strolled along the narrow path that led out of the village.

She glanced at Scorpio, who was a few steps ahead, his silhouette a soft contrast against the blue-gray sky. Today he had insisted on taking her to see the old museum, then the art gallery, and finally the lighthouse perched on the cliff. It was a typical Scorpio plan , casual yet thoughtful, unhurried yet with just the right amount of mystery.

It was a warm afternoon, and she could feel the salt of the ocean on her skin as they walked side by side. She adjusted the sleeves of her linen shirt , a loose, off-white thing, comfortable and perfect for the day. Scorpio wore his choice casual , a faded navy blue t-shirt that stretched just right over his shoulders, paired with a worn pair of beige cargo shorts. The simplicity of their clothes matched the village she now called home , a coastal town untouched by the chaos of city life. The gentle sway of the waves and the soft murmur of the wind were their constant companions.

They first stopped by the village's small museum. It was a humble building with walls filled with relics from past generations: old fishing tools, weathered photographs of the sea, and artifacts from the early days of the town. She wandered past a few displays, but her eyes kept drifting back to Scorpio. There was something about the way he moved through the museum , how he studied each exhibit, taking in the details with a kind of reverence that made her smile. She caught him gazing at a rusty harpoon on display, his fingers tracing the edge of a cracked photo frame.

"You know," she said, breaking the silence, "this town has always felt like a museum to me since I arrived . Each building, each person, seems to carry so much history." He turned to her, eyes thoughtful. "And some things stay hidden. Even the sea has its secrets."

She nodded, feeling the weight of his words. She had been fascinated by the secrets this town held , ever since she arrived. The way its stories lingered beneath the surface, just waiting to be uncovered. Scorpio was a keeper of some of those secrets, and she knew he could spend hours spinning tales if she asked.

After leaving the museum, they made their way to the art gallery, which was just a short walk from the town center. The gallery was modest, the kind of place that displayed local artists' work, capturing the essence of the coastal life. A few paintings lined the walls, some depicting stormy seas, others the quiet moments of fishing boats bobbing in the harbor at dawn. She paused in front of a portrait of a woman, her face half-obscured by a veil of sea mist.

"This one feels like it's hiding something," she mused, her finger lightly brushing the edge of the frame. "Like she knows something we don't." Scorpio's eyes flicked to the painting, his expression unreadable. "Maybe it's not about what's hidden. Maybe it's about what's been revealed." She tilted her head, intrigued by his response. "I think I know what you mean."

They lingered in the gallery for a while, but the call of the lighthouse soon tugged at them both. The path up to the lighthouse was an unfamiliar one for her , but for Scorpio it was one he had walked countless times, but he said today it felt different for him . The sun hung low in the sky, casting long shadows across the cliffside, and the salty air was thick with the scent of pine and brine.

At the top, the lighthouse stood tall, a silent guardian over the vast expanse of sea. The tower was white, with a red band around its midsection, its lens flashing every few seconds. She leaned against the stone railing, her gaze lost in the horizon, where the sea met the sky in a seamless blur of blue and gray. Scorpio stood next to her, close but not touching, as if they were both waiting for something , perhaps a word, or perhaps just the stillness of the moment.

They stayed there for a while, the only sounds being the soft crashing of waves below and the occasional call of a seagull. She found herself thinking about the simplicity of their lives in the village , the quiet days, the steady rhythm of the tide, the familiar faces. It wasn't much, but it was everything.

"Do you think we'll ever leave?" she asked suddenly, her voice barely a whisper above the wind. Scorpio's gaze shifted to her, his expression calm. "I don't know," he said, his voice low but steady. "Maybe it's not about leaving. Maybe it's about finding something you can carry with you."

She turned to him, meeting his eyes. There was a depth there, a kind of understanding that only someone who had spent years in the quiet, unhurried pace of the town could have. They were both grounded here, but also adrift , caught between the pull of the village and the vastness of the world beyond.

"I think I could stay forever," she said softly. Scorpio nodded, as if he had been expecting those words. They stood together in silence, watching the sunset as it painted the sky in shades of orange and purple.

As the evening settled in, they made their way back toward the village, their footsteps muffled by the soft earth. The streetlights flickered on, casting a warm glow over the cobblestones. They were hungry, and Scorpio suggested they grab something to eat at the local diner . A small, cozy spot known for its simple, yet satisfying meals.

Inside, the smell of freshly baked bread and grilled fish filled the air. Scorpio ordered a bowl of clam chowder and warm bread for her and for himself he chose a plate of fried cod with a side of potatoes. They sipped on cold, local beer, the conversation drifting between the mundane and the meaningful. The food was nothing fancy , just the kind of simple meal that tasted like home. She smiled, savoring each bite, feeling the comfort of the familiar around her. They rounded off the simple meal with a bowl of chocolate ice cream . She ordered an extra pack to take home for herself . She could binge on it if ever the thoughts of her ex returned and made her miserable.

The night was quiet, and as they left the diner, the stars above them seemed to echo the peace of the village. With Scorpio by her side, she felt as though she had everything she needed , this place, this moment, and the unspoken bond between them. It was enough.

CHAPTER EIGHT
A DAY IN THE QUIET FISHING TOWN

The week crawled by . Work kept me busy with only meeting Scorpio for a quick coffee in the evenings and more work at home trying to catch up to the new office backlogs . Then thankfully the weekend arrived . Along with the free hours , at nights would come the dreaded thoughts of a love long gone cold inside me .

It was one of those rare days when the town seemed to slow down, the rhythmic sound of the tide crashing against the rocks a gentle reminder of how still the world could be. The quiet fishing town we both worked in had its charm, but today, it was more serene than usual. Scorpio and I had planned a simple outing , no work, no rush, just a day spent in the peace of the countryside.

I met Scorpio in the late morning outside the small rental shop by the dock. The air was crisp and carried a hint of salt, as it always did by the water. He was dressed casually, as usual. He wore a well-worn navy blue T-shirt, its fabric softened by time and sun, paired with khaki shorts that hit just above his knees. His sneakers, scuffed from countless walks, added to the relaxed vibe of his outfit. His sunglasses perched high on his head, the sun only beginning to edge into its afternoon climb. The shades were a permanent fixture even when he wasn't using them to block out the light.

I had gone for something equally low-key. A soft gray hoodie, slightly oversized, and a pair of light denim jeans that were beginning to show their age with a few frayed edges. The sun was already warm, so I paired it with my favorite sneakers. That would be comfortable and easy for walking or cycling, which was exactly the plan for the day.

After a quick exchange of friendly banter, we rented bicycles from the small shop, the friendly owner grinning as she handed us the keys to the bikes. I always found it amusing how much the townspeople loved to chat, even when they were working. The shopkeeper was no exception . She gave us advice on the best routes and the quieter paths through the town, tips we always welcomed.

We hopped on the bikes, and the town revealed itself in its slow-moving pace. The path along the shore was perfect for cycling, the sound of the ocean creating an almost meditative soundtrack to our ride. Scorpio and I took turns taking the lead, laughing every time one of us tried to race ahead, only to be caught by the other. It was easy camaraderie, the kind of easy friendship that comes from years of knowing someone well enough to feel at home, even in the quietest of places.

Our destination was a small cove just outside of town, a secluded spot that the locals often used for picnics. As we approached, we could see the soft curve of the beach, the golden sand barely touched by footprints. We dismounted and rolled the bikes to a shaded spot under a row of tall, whispering trees, their leaves rustling gently in the breeze.

We spread out a blanket that Scorpio had packed earlier, and I was grateful for the simplicity of it all. No fuss, just the essentials: sandwiches, fruit, and a bottle of chilled white wine. Scorpio had outdone himself , this time he'd made the sandwiches himself, thick slices of sourdough bread stuffed with fresh tuna, lettuce, and a secret sauce that tasted like summer. She savored each bite, the salt of the sea mixing with the taste of the bread and tuna.

"Not bad, huh?" Scorpio asked, leaning back on his elbows and watching the waves gently lap at the shore. I grinned. "I think I might have to take you up on your offer to make lunch every weekend." He chuckled, looking pleased with himself. "I'll take that as a compliment."

We spent the afternoon talking about everything and nothing, the conversation flowing as effortlessly as the tide. Our lives were so intertwined by the work we did in the town that it felt natural to fall into these moments together, enjoying the space between words as much as the words themselves.

After lunch, we took a short walk along the beach, shoes abandoned by the water's edge. The sand was soft beneath our feet, and the occasional splash of cool water against our ankles felt like a small adventure. We kept the conversation light, sharing anecdotes from work and teasing each other about our various misadventures.

We talked about cycling routes we hadn't yet explored and the best places to eat in town, all the while laughing and catching up on things we'd never had time to discuss during the busy workweek.

As the day stretched on, we returned to the town by bike, the late afternoon light casting long shadows across the cobbled streets. We stopped at a small seafood restaurant by the docks for dinner. The place was cozy, with warm lighting and the rich aroma of grilled fish filling the air. We ordered the catch of the day, each dish expertly prepared with fresh herbs and a squeeze of lemon.

The evening settled in, and we ate slowly, savoring the meal and the quiet around us. There was something deeply satisfying about being in this little fishing town, far away from the chaos of the world. The simplicity of the day, from the bikes to the picnic, to the quiet dinner, made everything feel right.

As the sun finally dipped below the horizon, we paid the bill and walked back toward the quiet part of the town where our apartments were located. It was a peaceful walk, with the last remnants of light disappearing behind the silhouette of the hills. Scorpio and I fell into a comfortable silence, the kind that only happens after a day well spent.

When we reached the corner of my street, Scorpio turned to me with a grin. "Same time next week?" he asked, clearly not wanting the day to end. I smiled, feeling the warmth of the day still lingering in my bones. "You know it."

And with that, we parted ways, both of us content, knowing that our friendship and this quiet fishing town would always be there, waiting for the next adventure. As expected at home , the loneliness and loss set in again . Though I was thankful for Scorpio as a friend , it was just too soon to think about him romantically . I was just plain lucky to have met him and he gave me that impression too .

Nevertheless, our bodies are ruled by biology . I entered the shower for my leisurely night routine . As I hit the sheets , I sought the service of my toy . Ironically , each time I used it and neared the end ,the face that appeared in my mind was always my ex . I guess it's normal and it takes time for the body to rewrite the chemistry , and rewrite the connection with familiar pheromones . I do not blame my body . I will not blame myself .

As my eyes closed to sleep and my breathing slowed , I was jolted awake by my ex's voice " sweetheart, where are you " ? This voice it came into my soul with such clarity , it scared me to the core . Is he perhaps looking for me everywhere ? It's possible . Or is my soul searching him in spite of everything? Tears fell unknowingly. Let it fall . Let it wet . Let that end .

CHAPTER NINE
THE GIFT OF HEALING

The sound of soft hammering echoed from the sundeck of my small coastal apartment. Scorpio wiped his brow, setting the wooden mallet aside. His charcoal gray t-shirt was speckled with sawdust, and his olive-green cargo pants bore faint smudges of wood polish. He looked so hot . What is it that makes men look so attractive while they do chores like this around the house ? Dressed in the proper attire of course . The mid-morning sun had crept higher in the sky, casting golden light over the narrow space.

He took a step back to admire his work: a compact, sturdy dog house painted in shades of cream and sky blue, perfectly matching my apartment's nautical theme. The roof was slanted to withstand the coastal rain, and a small sign above the entry read "Sunny's Haven," hand-painted in elegant cursive. Scorpio smirked to himself, satisfied.

She was inside, humming to soft jazz playing from her speaker. She wore a breezy white cotton dress, the hem brushing her knees, her auburn hair loosely tied back. Her hands worked deftly in the small kitchen, slicing ripe tomatoes for a Caprese salad. On the counter, a jug of lemon-cucumber water sparkled in the sunlight streaming through the window. The smell of garlic and fresh basil wafted through the air, mingling with the salty breeze coming in from the sea.

When Scorpio knocked on the glass door to the sundeck, Ash turned, wiping her hands on a dish towel. "All done?" she asked, her voice light with curiosity."Almost," he said, stepping inside. "But you should see it now." She followed him outside, the sound of her sandals soft against the wooden floor. When her eyes landed on the dog house, she froze.

"Scorpio..." she began, her voice catching. "Wait. There's more." From behind the dog house, he lifted a small wicker basket lined with a fluffy blanket. Nestled inside was a tiny dachshund puppy, its chocolate-brown eyes wide and curious. Its short legs scrambled to stand as it let out a small, high-pitched bark. She gasped, her hands flying to her mouth. "His name's Sunny," Scorpio said, setting the basket down. "He's yours."

Tears welled in her eyes as she knelt down to pick up the puppy. Sunny's warm little body fit perfectly in her arms, his tail wagging furiously. "I don't know what to say," she whispered, burying her face in the puppy's soft fur. "You don't have to say anything," Scorpio replied, his voice gentle. "I just thought... you've been through a lot. Maybe he can help you feel like yourself again." She looked up at him, her expression still a mix of gratitude and disbelief. "You didn't have to do this." "I know," he said simply, a soft smile playing on his lips. "But I wanted to."

After settling Sunny into his new home, they moved inside. She insisted on cooking lunch, though Scorpio ended up helping anyway, as he often did. She handed him a cutting board and a bundle of fresh herbs while she worked on slicing bread for bruschetta.

"Sunny's a perfect name," She said as she drizzled olive oil over the bread. "Did you come up with it?" Scorpio shrugged, chopping parsley with practiced ease. "He just seemed like a Sunny to me. And I thought you could use a bit of sunshine in your life." She paused, her heart squeezing at his words. She didn't say anything, but her smile and her eyes said it all.

They sat down to eat at the small wooden table in her living room, the open windows letting in the sound of seagulls and distant waves. The meal was simple but comforting: bruschetta topped with juicy tomatoes, mozzarella, and basil, alongside a bowl of creamy mushroom soup. Scorpio poured them glasses of iced green tea, the mint leaves floating on top adding a refreshing touch.

Sunny toddled around their feet, his little paws pattering on the floor. Every now and then, she would lean down to give him a piece of bread crust or a quick scratch behind the ears. "This is the best meal I've had in weeks," Scorpio said, leaning back in his chair. "Because you made half of it," she teased, raising an eyebrow. He laughed, the sound warm and easy. "Fair point."

Later, as the sun dipped lower in the sky, she put on her favorite vinyl , a mellow folk album that always made her think of home. She lit a few candles and pulled out an old patchwork blanket for the couch.

Scorpio sat cross-legged on the floor, tossing a small ball for Sunny to chase. He stumbled after it with boundless enthusiasm, his ears flopping comically as she ran.

She watched them, her heart full in a way it hadn't been for a long time. Scorpio had been her anchor since she moved to the village, helping her navigate the unfamiliar rhythms of coastal life and supporting her as she healed from her last relationship. But this gesture , this was something else.

"You've done so much for me," she said softly, breaking the comfortable silence.Scorpio looked up, his expression unreadable for a moment before softening. "You deserve it, you know . You're stronger than you think. Sometimes you just need a reminder." She blinked back tears, her fingers idly tracing the edge of her tea mug. "Thank you," she said, her voice steady. "For everything." She felt teary eyed today . Goodness . He held her gaze, and for a moment, the air between them seemed to shift. But then Sunny barked, pouncing on the ball with triumphant glee, and the moment passed

As the evening deepened, Scorpio prepared to leave. He stood by the door, his jacket slung over one shoulder, while she cradled Sunny in her arms. "Don't let him boss you around," he said, grinning. "He may be small, but he's got a big personality." She laughed. "I think I'll manage."

He hesitated for a moment, then reached out to gently ruffle her hair. "Take care of yourself . And let me know if you need anything. "I will," she promised, her smile genuine. As he walked down the stairs and out into the night, she stood by the door, watching until he disappeared from view. Sunny squirmed in her arms, licking her cheek and making her laugh.

For the first time in what felt like forever, she felt a glimmer of hope. Maybe, just maybe, this little village and the people in it, could be the fresh start she needed. It all depends on our attitude . Like Scorpio , when we choose positive , we put good energy into everything we do . We speak in words that strengthen us and others . We think of actions that may help in move us and others forward . Scorpio effortlessly created a meaningful and joyful world for me with just a few actions . Without him it may have been a long and tedious climb to the summit . Who knows . With that little bit of help I will create a new reality free of pain and memories , moment by moment , choice after choice , thought after thought . Grateful .

Tomorrow and all other days I will strive to wake up with a smile , see the good in everything, and will try to remind myself that every moment is a hidden new opportunity to create a good life .

CHAPTER TEN
THE FESTIVAL GLOW

This fishing town rarely broke its tranquil rhythm, its life dictated by the sea and sky. But tonight, the annual town festival had transformed the usually somber docks into a wonderland of twinkling lights, vibrant stalls, and laughter that mingled with the salty sea breeze. Scorpio leaned against his bike , waiting at the corner of her street.

He glanced at his watch, then back to the small apartment . When she finally stepped out, his breath hitched for a moment. She wore a simple, flowing dress in shades of teal that mirrored the sea. A light scarf draped over her shoulders, and her hair, usually tied back, cascaded freely. Scorpio thought she looked beautiful, though he'd never say it aloud.

"Sorry, I took a bit longer," she said, her voice soft and apologetic."You're right on time," Scorpio assured her. "Ready for some fun?" She hesitated. "I think so. Thanks for inviting me, by the way. I've never been to a town festival before." It's a long time that I pillion ride a bike too . Scorpio smiled. "Then we've got a lot to cover." Riding in close proximity to Scorpio didn't pose a problem at least for now .They arrived at the festival scene .

The streets leading to the docks were alive with music and chatter. Strings of fairy lights crisscrossed above, illuminating clusters of people browsing handmade crafts, tasting local delicacies, and gathering around musicians. Scorpio led her through the crowd with an easy confidence, his broad shoulders clearing a path as she faithfully trailed behind, her wide eyes taking in everything.

"Hungry?" he asked, stopping at an open-air food stall where the scent of grilled seafood temptingly mingled with the sweetness of fresh-baked pastries . "I could eat," she replied, a small smile tugging at her lips.

They ordered fried calamari, crisp and golden, served with a tangy garlic aioli. Scorpio also grabbed a bowl of his favorite clam chowder for both , while she eyed the display of desserts. "Those look amazing," she murmured, pointing to the lemon tarts dusted with powdered sugar.

"You've got good taste," Scorpio said, adding a tart to their order. They found a quiet spot near the edge of the dock, where wooden benches overlooked the moonlit waves. Ash took a cautious bite of the tart, and her expression softened into one of delight. "This is incredible," she said. "Told you," Scorpio replied, his tone casual but his gaze warm as he watched her relax.

The distant strains of carnival music drew their attention, and Scorpio gestured toward the Ferris wheel. "You up for it?" She hesitated, as its been a long time since she had done a Ferris wheel , but then nodded. "Why not?"

The Ferris wheel, adorned with multicolored lights, loomed over the festival like a sentinel. They joined the line, and Scorpio handed the attendant a couple of tickets. Once inside the small, swaying gondola, she gripped the metal bar tightly. "Not a fan of heights huh ?" Scorpio asked. "It's not that," she said, her voice barely above a whisper. "Just... trying out new things after a gap of time make me nervous sometimes."

As the wheel began to turn, she tried to focus on the view rather than her racing thoughts. The entire town stretched below them, its twinkling lights reflected in the dark water. Scorpio didn't press her to talk, sensing her need for space. When the gondola reached its apex, the ride paused, leaving them suspended. She finally exhaled. "It's beautiful up here," she admitted grudgingly. "Yeah, it is," Scorpio said, though his eyes weren't on the view but on her.

She caught his gaze and looked away, feeling a blush creep into her cheeks. "I haven't felt this... peaceful in a long time," she confessed. "Good," Scorpio said simply. "You deserve it."

When they stepped off the Ferris wheel, she felt lighter, as though she'd left a piece of her burden behind. They wandered through the market stalls, where she admired handcrafted jewelry , beautiful shells and colorful scarves. She always had a fascination for shells . Scorpio bought her a small, intricately carved wooden keychain shaped like a seashell. "Something to remember tonight," he said as he handed it to her. She smiled, instantly this time. "Thank you."

As the night wore on, they stopped at more food stalls, sampling grilled corn on the cob slathered with butter and a savory seafood paella served in small paper bowls. Scorpio pointed out people he knew, sharing stories that made her laugh for the first time in what felt like forever.

When they reached the central square, a live band was playing folk music. Couples danced under the string lights, their movements as fluid as the waves. Scorpio turned to her and offered his hand. "Dance with me?" She hesitated, but his patient smile melted her reservations. "Okay," she said, placing her hand in his.

Scorpio wasn't an expert dancer, but he led with a confidence that made it easy for her to follow. As they moved, she let the music and the moment carry her. For the first time in years, she wasn't thinking about what she'd lost, but what she was beginning to find. When the song ended, Scorpio didn't let go immediately, his hand lingering on hers. "You did great," he said. She laughed softly. "You're not bad yourself."

The festival was winding down when they decided to call it a night. Scorpio took her back to her apartment on the bike. The streets were now quiet but still aglow with the remnants of the evening's magic. "Thanks for tonight," she said as they reached her door. "I didn't realize how much I needed this." "Anytime," Scorpio replied. "I'm glad you came."

She hesitated before leaning in to press a light but firm kiss to his cheek. "Goodnight, Scorpio." "Goodnight, fun girl ," he said, watching as she stepped inside, the door closing softly behind her. As Scorpio walked back to his bike , he couldn't help but smile. It had been a simple night, but he knew it was the start of something much bigger for both of them.

CHAPTER ELEVEN
HEALING TIDES

Without her knowing it , the emotional connection with Scorpio was enhancing and enriching her sensory details of how she was now viewing Scorpio. She now began to feel that they may now anytime move forward from the boundaries of just a deep friendship.

Originally she had chosen the fishing town for its quiet charm and anonymity. The waves of the sea seemed to echo her own turbulent emotions , always moving, yet never truly still. Now every morning, she woke to the cries of gulls and the rhythmic splash of water against the harbor's wooden posts. The apartment she was given perched above a small embankment, with windows that framed the view of bobbing boats and weathered fishermen hauling their nets.

This was supposed to be her sanctuary, a place to rebuild herself after a relationship that had left her raw and uncertain. For months, she avoided entanglements of any kind. She was here to heal, not to fall apart again. That resolve wavered the day she met Scorpio.

They met almost daily now , saw him most of the days on the beach during her morning walks. The tide had now receded, leaving behind shimmering pools of water in the grooves of the sand. Today she was crouched by a tide-pool, watching tiny crabs skitter under rocks, when a wet nose nudged her arm.

Startled, she looked up to see Scorpios dog staring at her with wagging enthusiasm. Come here!" Scorpios deep voice would call .

He was jogging toward her with a casual, rugged charm. His dark hair was tousled by the sea breeze, and his lean, muscular frame moved with an easy confidence. He was smiling, the kind of smile that could disarm anyone. Was her heart wavering ?

"I'm so sorry," he said as he reached her, slightly out of breath. "He has a habit of saying hello to everyone with his nose " "It's fine," she replied, laughing softly as she scratched the Labrador behind the ears. "He's sweet."

Their paths now seemed to cross often. Sometimes it was deliberate , like when Scorpio invited her to coffee, or when she asked if he wanted to walk the dog together. Other times, it was serendipitous, like running into each other at the farmer's market or on the pier.

Scorpio wasn't like anyone she had ever known. He was patient and kind, never pressing her for details about her past but always willing to listen when she wanted to share. He worked on his own and his stories about life on the town fascinated her. He had an easy way of making her laugh, his dry humor and mischievous grin breaking through her guarded demeanor always . Where is this all headed to , she wondered .

Over time, her feelings for him deepened. They spent evenings cooking together in her small kitchen, sharing meals of fresh seafood and crusty bread. They sat on the pier late at night, sipping modest beer and watching the stars.

But no matter how close they became, she kept a piece of herself locked away. She was afraid to let him in completely, afraid of the vulnerability that came with intimacy.

One evening , Scorpio invited her to dinner, but she suggested they meet at her apartment instead. She felt ready , so ready to take a step forward, even if it terrified her. The day of their dinner, she spent hours preparing. Her apartment was modest but cozy, with modest furniture and walls adorned with watercolor paintings of the sea. She set the table with her best plates, lit a few candles, and chose soft jazz to play in the background.

For dinner, she prepared shrimp pasta with a light garlic cream sauce and roasted vegetables. The scents filled the apartment, mingling with the salty breeze wafting in from the harbor. She chose a navy-blue dress that skimmed her knees, pairing it with a cream cardigan. Her dark hair was swept into a loose bun, a few tendrils framing her face.

When Scorpio arrived, his dog trotted in first, his tail wagging as he sniffed around the apartment searching for Sunny my puppy . Scorpio followed, holding a bottle of Merlot and a small box tied with twine. "Something sweet for dessert," he said, grinning as he handed her the box."Thank you," she said, her cheeks warming. She gestured for him to sit as she poured the wine.

Dinner was a leisurely affair. The wine loosened their tongues, and their laughter filled the room. Scorpio recounted a story about a particularly mischievous dolphin that had stolen fish from his boating trip and she shared a memory of her childhood visits to the ocean.

The food was simple but delicious, and the candles cast a golden glow over the table. She became acutely aware of the way Scorpio's knee brushed hers under the table, the way his fingers lingered just a moment too long when he passed her the wine bottle.

After dinner, they moved to the couch, bringing the tiramisu and the last of the wine with them. Both dogs curled up at their feet, their soft snores a comforting background noise.

The air between them grew thick with unspoken tension. Scorpio leaned back, his arm resting on the back of the couch. She felt the heat of his gaze, her pulse quickening as their eyes met. "You've created something beautiful here," he said, gesturing around the room. "It feels like you."

She smiled, her fingers brushing the rim of her wine glass. "It's taken time. But I'm starting to feel like myself again." "Good," he said softly, leaning closer. "Because I've wanted to say this for a while now , I care about you, fun girl . More than just a friend." Her breath caught, her heart pounding. "I care about you too," she whispered. Scorpio reached out, cupping her cheek with his hand. "May I?" She nodded, and he closed the distance between them, his lips capturing hers in a kiss that was full of longing.

They stumbled toward her bedroom, their movements unhurried but filled with purpose. His dog , sensing he was no longer needed, trotted off to the kitchen , hotly followed by my puppy . In the dim light of the bedroom, Scorpio took his time, his fingers tracing the curve of her jaw before sliding down her arms. Her cardigan slipped from her shoulders, revealing the smooth expanse of her skin. "You're so beautiful," he murmured, his voice husky. She felt a warmth spread through her chest. She reached for his shirt, her fingers fumbling with the buttons. When it finally fell open, she ran her hands over the firm planes of his chest, marveling at the way his muscles tensed under her touch.

Their clothes fell away, piece by piece, until there was nothing between them. The scent of wine, the salty tang of the sea air, and the faint musk of their mingling bodies filled the room. Scorpio was gentle, but only at first , his movements deliberate as he explored every inch of her. She felt her barriers crumbling, the weight of her past lifting with every touch, every crunchy kiss.

Afterward, they lay tangled in the sheets, their breaths mingling in the quiet of the room. Scorpio traced lazy circles on her bare shoulder, his other hand resting lightly on her waist. "I didn't think

I could feel this way again," she admitted, her voice barely above a whisper.

He pressed a kiss to her forehead. "Neither did I. But here we are." The sound of the waves outside matched the steady rhythm of their breaths. For the first time in months , she felt whole. She turned to Scorpio, her fingers brushing his cheek.

"Stay," she said softly . He smiled, pulling her closer. "Always."As the night stretched on, she drifted off in his arms, the weight of her past replaced by the promise of a new beginning

CHAPTER 12
THE MORNING AFTER

The first light of dawn crept softly through the bedroom window, casting a gentle glow across the room. She stirred, the warmth of Scorpio's body beside her grounding her to the earth in a way she hadn't felt in months . His arm was draped protectively over her waist, and the scent of his cologne mixed with the lingering fragrance of their night together. For a moment, everything felt still and perfect, as though the world outside her small apartment had faded away.

She inhaled deeply, savoring the closeness of him. His breathing was steady, the rise and fall of his chest in sync with hers. It was a comfort she hadn't realized she needed, a safe space where the noise of her past no longer lingered. She shifted slightly, her head resting on his chest, listening to the rhythmic sound of his heartbeat.

Scorpio stirred beside her, his hand tightening briefly around her waist before he pulled her closer, his lips brushing against her forehead. "Morning," he murmured, his voice husky with sleep.

"Morning," she replied, her heart fluttering in her chest. She could still taste him on her lips, feel the warmth of his skin against hers, and the connection they had shared only hours before. He smiled, lifting his head to meet her gaze. His stormy eyes softened as he ran his fingers through her hair. "You okay?" She nodded, her fingers tracing the line of his jaw. "Yeah. I think I might actually be more than okay."

A playful smirk tugged at the corner of his lips as he leaned in for a lingering kiss, deep and slow, their bodies pressing closer again. The heat between them flared instantly, a quiet hunger rising that neither of them had yet shaken off from the night before. His hands roamed, brushing over the curve of her back, pulling her closer until she felt the undeniable warmth of his desire. The world outside their small bubble of intimacy seemed distant, as if the morning was simply another continuation of the connection they had begun the night before.

She parted from him, breathless. She smiled, her fingers tracing his chest. "As much as I would love to stay like this," she said, her voice soft but playful, "we do have to get up at some point." He grinned, reluctant to pull away but clearly agreeing. "Guess you're right. How about breakfast first, then church? We're not far from the chapel, right?"

She nodded, propping herself up on one elbow to look out the window. The small town stretched out before them, the early morning mist still clinging to the rooftops. "Yeah, it's just a short walk. I thought it'd be nice to go today. It's Sunday, after all. Scorpio rolled onto his back with a sigh, pulling her against him once more. "Sounds good. But breakfast first, and then maybe a nap later."

The smell of sizzling bacon and fresh eggs filled the apartment as she moved around the kitchen, humming softly to herself. She had decided to go all out for breakfast, something hearty to start the day. Scorpio had claimed the coffee pot, his hands expertly preparing two mugs of rich, dark coffee. He set them down on the small wooden table by the window, the steam rising from the cups.

"You want me to help with anything?" he asked, leaning against the counter and watching her move with ease around the small kitchen. She glanced over her shoulder, offering him a smile. "You can set the table if you want, and maybe grab that fruit bowl from the counter." "On it," Scorpio said, a playful gleam in his eye as he moved to follow her directions.

She couldn't help but notice how effortlessly they worked together, how his presence in her space felt so right. They'd only known each other for a few months, but it felt like a lifetime. The rhythm of their morning was gentle, intimate in its simplicity. They joked and laughed, the mundane moments of cooking breakfast feeling like a shared experience they would remember for years to com

Once the food was ready, they sat down to eat, the sun fully risen now, casting warm beams of light across the room. They enjoyed the simple pleasure of good food, good company, and the ease of being with someone who made everything feel natural.

As they ate, they shared a quiet conversation about the upcoming week. Scorpio mentioned his plans for a deep-sea fishing trip with some of the local crew and told her about a painting he had started working on , a seascape of the harbor at sunrise that was beginning to take shape in the studio. " Wow " , that's wonderful , she said

"I like hearing your compliments " Scorpio said, his voice tender as he reached across the table to squeeze her hand. "It's... different from anything I've ever known. It's not just the work you do, but how it makes others feel. I can see it in your eyes."

She blushed slightly, her heart swelling with warmth. "Thanks," she whispered, squeezing his hand in return. "It's been a while since I really complimented anyone."

The conversation lulled, and for a moment, they just sat in the comfortable silence, the faint sound of the waves outside the only interruption.

After breakfast, they dressed in quiet comfort. She opted for a soft, navy-blue sweater and jeans, while Scorpio wore his usual jeans and a well-worn plaid shirt. They walked hand in hand down the cobblestone streets of the fishing town, the morning sunlight warming the chill in the air. Both dogs trotted beside them, his tail wagging happily as he took in the familiar sights of the town.

The quaint church was nestled at the end of the main street, its white stone facade standing out against the vibrant green of the surrounding trees. The bell tower chimed softly, signaling the beginning of Sunday service. She glanced at Scorpio, her fingers tightening around his.

"Ready?" she asked softly, her voice low with the weight of unspoken emotions. He gave her a reassuring smile. "Always." They entered the church together, the scent of incense and polished wood greeting them. The congregation was small, but the atmosphere was peaceful and reverent. They found seats near the back, because of the dogs , now lying quietly by their feet. As the service began, she felt a quiet sense of gratitude wash over her.

For the first time in a long while, she wasn't carrying the weight of her past with her. There, in the quiet, surrounded by the hum of prayer and the soft hymns, she could breathe deeply, knowing she had found a place of peace. Scorpio's hand found hers once again, his thumb brushing softly over her knuckles.

As the service drew to a close, they stood together, their voices joining with the rest of the congregation in the final prayer. Her heart was light, the morning's simple moments reaffirming what she had known since meeting Scorpio: healing wasn't just about moving on; it was about finding the people and moments that made her feel whole again. And with him, she felt like she was finally, beautifully whole.

This episode was like a natural destination for her and Scorpio's journey, offering a peaceful morning of connection and shared experiences.

CHAPTER THIRTEEN
ALL THIS ANGER , WAS ONCE YOUR LOVE

Time slips through your fingers , while you are holding on to the things that do not matter .

Change is painful . Growth is even more . But is there anything more painful than staying lodged like a broken kite , in a place where you clearly don't belong . Most people never heal . Because they do not remove themselves from darkness .

Simple souls they may be . But they get entangled in somebody's drama. They stand rooted to that spot . Even after breaking up , they replay those betraying scenarios in their head . Over and over again . Brooding , thinking what ifs , determining the time limes of betrayal , thinking what they did wrong . You did not do anything wrong . You just did everything right . And that was the problem . Doing everything too perfectly.

You thought you were happy . You thought that this toxic love made you happy . In time you will realize that love isn't always enough . To be in love doesn't always mean that you are happy , or you will stay happy . This so called love sometimes continues to exist in your mind , even after knowing that someone you loved has hurt you . The thrilling and bizarre truth is , that's the time you have to break up with the betrayer .

You have to part yourself from the person you love while you are still in love with them . The reason being that , there is a very thin line between hate and love . Do it while this is strong . For your recovery will be faster . Your soul will make you understand that and you will feel it deep inside you , that however much your love is , and even if you are ready to forgive , it will never ever be the same again . Because now you know , who they are . This point , or at some point , you have to let them go . The sooner it's done the better .

A strong woman , sometimes allows herself to willingly immerse herself in her solitude, but then she rises from the ashes of life . Eventually , we all are looking towards making our life worthwhile . Collecting the remaining fragments of our soul . Finding a purpose . Constantly trying to improve on our imperfections . While we are at it , we are also trying to dream up a good life and striving to make it happen .

Then comes along something that stops us on our tracks . A relationship . We are swept up on our feet . Purpose forgotten . Just living to fulfill the others dreams , making them happy . It doesn't matter to us then that our life moves too fast or slow . We are with somebody . And their pace of life , their desires , wishes , become ours . Then something shatters that bubble . And the heart always comes back . Back to you .

Such a time is mine now . Everything is passing by . Everyone seems to be together and in bliss . Except me . It seems everyone is together, except me . It's seems everybody even just around the corner are deliriously happy . They look the perfect picture . But I am alone. But not unhappy . This reality finally hits everyone who is on a breakup . The reality now depends on the routine. The routine where only you matters .

The abusers face sometimes flashes on to my thoughts . But it seems blurry now . Like a blurred photograph . The brain does this favor for you . Assisting you to blur and eventually block out situations , faces and people who are associated with any kind of hurt .

But it doesn't let you block out conversations . It reminds you of the sounds of a laugh , reminds you of teasing dialogues , reminds you of compliments , pledges of I love you, you're stunning , you are amazing .

If I feel sleepy he said. " Catch fire babe . Get me in a good mood to play. I ask him 'do you want more'? 'Yes more'. ' The night is still young, my sweetheart . When he says that, I take him in my hot wet mouth. Then the story repeats itself. We sleep tight after playing this marathon. Days, weeks, months and years went by. Then I knew everything , the mask finally slipped and then the rose bubble burst, forever .

Now it seems like another life I had . But , there is always a but isn't it ? Have to heal . I haven't reached there yet . But I'm on my way . I'll get there . You will get there too. Be resolute .

So take on your fears and throw them in the sea . Watch the beautiful dawn break , at the end of every night . Feel the darkness gone from you . In the center of your turbulent heart , there is a place of calm . A place that will not be affected by change or loss of love . Where fear has no place . When you walk towards that place , fear runs away . Now go look for that place within you .

As I stand on the other side of this journey, I realize now that this wasn't just about leaving an abusive relationship—it was about reclaiming my life. The decision to go no contact was the first real step I took toward freedom, a silent profound act of self-care. Each day that followed that brought me clarity and healing, though it wasn't always linear. Some days were consumed by silence , sadness , gloom and doubt, while others were filled with a newfound sense of confidence and strength.

The silence that once felt like a punishment turned into my greatest friend . In it , I found the space to heal, the courage to reflect on my self worth, and the resolve to never return to a life where my identity was compromised and submerged . Slowly, I could put together the pieces of my shattered self . The difference was that , this time, it was stronger , each piece rebuilt with a new wisdom, self-compassion, and unshakable boundaries.

In the process of rebuilding, I learned to live again . Not just survive. I pursued passions I had forgotten, reconnected with long lost true friends, and embraced the everyday joy of small victories. Most surprisingly , I discovered that life beyond the pain is not only possible but it's beautiful. I've learned to trust my instincts again, to value my peace above all else, and to understand that the journey to healing is one of resilience and self-discovery.

God exists in his essence in this universe

The uniqueness of the Almighty is actually an indication of our powerlessness in the scale of things .

If there's white there's also black and gray...

If there is day there is night

We live in a universe full of internal and external contradictions

There is light and there is darkness...

If only humans can illuminate the darkness with some good deeds , then they won't condemn their souls to darkness with their evil designs .

But as they say , let's not forget , that the darkest moment at night is undoubtedly the time before dawn breaks the sky into shimmering colors .

Humans are wrong but then , we have our truths too

We all have hope , some have love , and some may get companionship. Whatever we get , it's valuable , to live in this moment . And as long as we live , we will live in the shade of gratitude , companionship and sometimes love .

This is not the end , it's a beginning. A beginning of a life lived , free from the shadows of control and manipulation. To anyone reading this, remember that the path to breaking free is your own, and though the road may be difficult, the destination is worth every step. You are capable of rebuilding, of healing, and of rising stronger than ever before. When the replacement for your love arrives , you will forget what you lost .

This is your moment to get yourself Untethered.

—R.M

Author : Mendez , is of Portuguese and Spanish descent , and of Anglo Indian origins . She holds a Masters in Aviation from Geneva , and lives in the Middle East as an Aviation professional . This is her partly real life journey , of an escape from an abuser , her self imposed no contact and eventual healing .

About the Author

The author Ms.Mendez of Portugese descent , and Anglo Indian origin , is an Aviation professional living in the Middle East .

9 798230 860242